Neversays

Neversays

25 Phrases You Should Never Ever Say
to Keep Your Job and Friends

Randi Bryant

Library of Congress Control Number:		2017916255
ISBN:		
	Hardcover	978-1-5434-6017-9
	Softcover	978-1-5434-6018-6
	eBook	978-1-5434-6019-3

Print information available on the last page.

Rev. date: 12/12/2017

To order additional copies of this book, contact:
Xlibris
1-888-795-4274
www.Xlibris.com
Orders@Xlibris.com
762153

Contents

We allow our ignorance to prevail upon us and make us think we can survive alone, alone in patches, alone in groups, alone in races, even alone in genders.

—Maya Angelou

Not everything that is faced can be changed; but nothing can be changed until it is faced.

—James Baldwin

ABOUT THE AUTHOR

Randi Bryant's sharp wit and insightful analysis find their roots in the combination of her professional endeavors, educational coursework and her personal experience as a Black woman in America.

The earliest seeds were planted as Randi spent dozens of holidays sitting around a large wooden table with a racially, religiously, politically, socio-economically and culturally diverse cast of characters debating and bonding over everything from the consumption of pork, the merits of "Reagon-nomics" and the space program. In the years since, those seeds grew as Randi became fascinated with the way people -- particularly those who are culturally different -- interact, communicate, work and live together.

This fascination was heightened and refined through her graduate studies at the College of William & Mary which focused on how to maximize learning for diverse student populations. She found this work particularly meaningful due to her own educational experience in which oftentimes she was the only minority in her entire school.

Randi's professional experience furthered her interest in, and commitment to, cultural understanding and communications. She first worked as a high school teacher in the most diverse public high school in Virginia. Randi then started her doctorate studies at the University of Virginia focusing on the way adults best learn and retain information. While there, she started developing training materials for newly developed technologies during the dot.com era. The excitement of these opportunities lured her to begin working with technology companies on the training and communications surrounding their emerging technologies. She then joined a high-tech company in Northern Virginia where she quickly rose to become the Director of Training and Development.

In 2001, Randi founded and still operates a corporate training company which allowed her to travel the country educating companies, executives and employees on topics including anti-discrimination, communication in a diverse work environment, and how to capitalize on a diverse workforce. Her clients have included McDonalds, Comcast, SAIC, Department of Energy, Department of State, Defense Advanced Research Agency, Starwood Hotels & Resorts and AT&T. Her experiences have reminded her of how uninformed people in the United States are about racial, gender and cultural issues – and how scared they are to discuss them.

Randi also writes a popular blog, Beatnik24.com, that often addresses issues of race, diversity and communication. She is also a sought after speaker on diversity issues.

randibryant.com

ABOUT THE ILLUSTRATOR

Ron Rogers, a longtime artist and illustrator, is a native of Richmond, Virginia. He has worked at newspapers across the country and especially enjoys drawing cartoons.

A brilliant and eclectic body of work! Randi takes on exceedingly complex issues that have been central to race, class and gender divisiveness that leaves the reader feeling hopeful and inspired that "finally" there's something to elegantly address these hot button issues that continue to polarize American society. A remarkable read for everyone to apply at work, home or elsewhere!

Kevin Brown
President/CEO
Vector Holding Group

Ms Bryant is a true master....she has found a clever way to help the reader deal with a subject that many feel uncomfortable discussing. This is a must read for anyone serious about diversity in the workplace.

Never Says takes an honest look at the world of stereotypes. It gives you actionable steps to bettering communication and creating an environment of understanding, which results in improved productivity. I highly recommend Never Says for business leaders.

Mr. Cedric Jones,
McDonald's, USA LLC
Vice President, GM

Randi's unique voice brings a fresh perspective to the diversity and inclusion dialogue in corporate America. From the boardroom, to the shop floor -- and all work environments in between -- *The Neversays* provides a useful tool for increasing understanding and improving communications in the workplace. Too often ignorance about and discomfort with diversity issues can lead to lost productivity, unwanted attrition and legal exposure. Randi and *The Neversays* provide practical advice and helpful guidance for avoiding these problems.

Tami Martin
Bryant Consulting Group
Vice President

"Diversity and Inclusion" has become popular in today's vernacular. Randi has treated the topic in a way that is unique and finally practical. If this topic is of interest to you in any remote way, please read this book.

Everyone is talking about D and I these days. Randi has taken the topic and provided a fresh approach to this important but over-worked concept. This book is well written and will hold your attention.

Erik Moore
Founder and Managing Director,
Base Ventures
(Early Stage Tech Investment Fund)

Finally, a book addresses the ideas of diversity and inclusivity in a practical and approachable manner so that every person can learn and grow; and every organization build closer and more productive teams.NEVERSAYS is timely and necessary for today's modern workforce.

Michael MOUSSA-ADAMO

Ambassador of the Gabonese Republic
to the USA, Mexico and to Haiti

some people
when they hear
your story.
contract.
others
upon hearing
your story,
expand...
-Nayyirah Waheed

This is Randi. She expands and expands and expands with every story told to her. She is both a messenger and a voice for the underrepresented and the marginalized among us.I first met Randi Bryant when she taught at Wakefield High school. Wakefield, with students from over 87 countries of origin and a population that is 70% free and reduced lunch, is a diverse and beautiful place to teach. During her time here as an English teacher, she was absolutely dedicated to ensuring that the curriculum in her department was designed to create an inclusive environment for our students. She has continued on her quest to create environments where all people feel included.

Jina Davidson
Art Department Chair
Photography/AP Art History/AP Studio Art Teacher
Wakefield High School

PREFACE

This book does not come from the sanitized part of me. This book comes from a place where frustration and hope coexist.

My years traveling the United States to help diverse populations communicate more effectively showed me that we are a nation of mostly well-intentioned, good people, who have no idea how to communicate with those who are different from us. More often than not, we live with, socialize with, and get our K-12 education with people who are very similar to us.

When we go away to college or join the workforce, we are suddenly immersed in environments where we are expected to communicate and work with people who are culturally foreign to us. We are placed in diverse environments, provided with elaborate diversity and inclusivity mission statements, all without having the knowledge and skill set to work with people who come from different cultural or experiential backgrounds. Even if our intentions are good; our experiences and training haven't prepared us to communicate effectively.

So we choose to self-segregate and limit our communication with those who are less culturally familiar, which results in ineffective teams, isolating work environments, and failed organizations. And sometimes when we do communicate, we use language that is not culturally competent nor compassionate, which causes hurt feelings, and negative work environments for us; and also results in lawsuits, low performance and high attrition for organizations.

Effective communication is a skill. One must learn how to communicate in a way that is inclusive, not exclusive; with language that creates bonds and not barriers.

Neversays is a practical guide that quickly teaches us the biggest cultural communication pitfalls, how to avoid them, and an explanation of why the phrases are offensive.

If you would like to improve your communication skills, work in a more cohesive environment, improve your existing work and social relationships, and develop new relationships, I am confident that *Neversays* will help you

INTRODUCTION

Good folks say dumb stuff. Most of us aren't racist, sexist, elitist, or homophobic: we're just ignorant. The majority of us just don't know how to talk to and interact with people who are different from us, so sometimes we end up making mistakes.

Consider the communication snafus that occur in your own home: you guys know and love one another intimately, but you still unintentionally say things to one another that are upsetting. Can you imagine what happens in a workplace or any public space where folks from all different backgrounds, carrying their own unconscious biases, are thrown together?

After twenty years of facilitating courses centered on the subjects of diversity and communication, I am passionate in my belief that most of the tension, misunderstanding, conflict, and anger in America are the result of our incompetence in and fear of dealing with difference.

OUR DIVERSE WORLD

The United States is a pluralistic society: an ever-increasing mixture of cultures, languages, nationalities, races, religions, political beliefs, sexual orientations, educational attainment, and income levels. Consider the following:

- Census data tells us that by 2050, there will be no racial or ethnic majority in our country.
- Between the years 2000 and 2050, new immigrants and their children will account for 83 percent of the growth in the working-age population.
- On June 26, 2015, the U.S. Supreme Court ruled that the U.S. Constitution guarantees the right for same-sex couples to marry in all fifty states.
- About 57 percent of women, eighteen and over, participate in the workforce.

These trends are accelerating. Interacting within a diverse society is a "new norm" to which we must all adjust.

RESPONDING TO OUR CHANGING WORLD

In an effort to adjust to our changing world, companies, schools, and organizations have made great strides to ensure that their populations are reflective of our broader society. They have hired chief diversity officers, spent billions to teach tolerance, and written elaborate diversity and inclusion mission statements.

Companies have focused on diversity in hiring yet have neglected to pay similar attention to the integration and cultivation of these people once hired. Consequently, people are unhappy, disengaged, and teamwork and collaboration suffer while attrition increases. When these employees leave, it reflects a loss of institutional and personal investment. Studies show that companies cite attrition as their second-biggest business concern. And concurrently, employees cite working in a positive work environment and feeling engaged to be among the top five reasons why they would stay in an organization.

Organizations are starting to realize that mere diversity simply does not equal inclusion. Diversity means having a variety of races, genders, cultures, sexual orientations, and capabilities represented within your ranks. Inclusion means creating an environment where all these people feel as if they belong and are accepted. Effective communication is the bridge from diversity to inclusion.

Diversity + Compassionate Communication = Inclusive Environment

Diversity without inclusivity equals failure for any organization. Consider Tiplee Corporation.

Tiplee Corporation is the largest employer in Kentucky. It employs over six thousand employees in the state. Their leadership has touted the interest and importance of diversity within the workforce. Citing the increasing diversity of their client base and suggesting it would be good to mirror that diversity in its workforce, Tiplee has invested heavily in recruiting a diverse pool of candidates, yet it continues to struggle with the retention of these highly talented individuals. About 50 percent of Tiplee's African American employees depart within three years. For Latino employees, the numbers are even more troubling. This attrition is a huge business issue for Tiplee. As with every departing employee, there is a corresponding loss of both intellectual and financial capital, as well as, the time invested in recruiting and training that employee.

IS THIS A BIG DEAL, REALLY?

In short, yes.

> ➤ According to the EEOC, there were 88,778 discrimination lawsuits in the workplace in 2014 alone.
> ➤ Communication issues, particularly with a boss, are cited as the either number three -- or among the top three reasons people quit their jobs.
> ➤ Regardless of how well you do your job or what degrees you have, being able to get along with others in our very diverse workplace is essential. Most CEOs and hiring professionals list the ability to work with others as one of the most important traits when it comes to job security.
> ➤ Life is just easier when you aren't pissing people off.

WHY DON'T DIVERSITY EFFORTS WORK?

Diversity is about numbers (how many diverse employees we can hire). Inclusivity is about people, integration, and engagement. For diversity and inclusivity efforts to work, you must focus on preparing the people; you must provide real tools and arm people to interact effectively and compassionately in a diverse community.

An identity group is the shared social characteristics, such as worldview, language, values, and ideological system that evolve from membership in a group.

Most diversity programs and trainings are focused on ideas and concepts, such as tolerance. They were designed to instill principles of character, such as accepting all people, regardless of difference; however, these programs failed to provide a guidebook about how to do that exactly. Consequently, well-meaning people find themselves in bad communication situations, tense relationships, and uncomfortable or even hostile work environments. This is not because of a lack of desire but rather because of a lack of exposure.

More often than not, we socialize with, educate ourselves with, work with, and otherwise live our lives surrounded by family, friends, and neighbors who are very similar to us. A recent CNN poll found that four out of ten white Americans do not have any nonwhite friends. Things aren't dramatically different for any other identity group

Consequently, most of us are ill-prepared to deal with people different from us. We go off to our schools, jobs, and organizations armed with the appropriate technical knowledge on how to perform required tasks but almost zero knowledge or experience on how to work with the diverse community in which we have suddenly found ourselves.

Not surprisingly, mistakes happen on the individual level, which trigger big consequences. Let's consider Bob's story.

Bob grew up surrounded by a large family in a small town in Utah. After graduating from high school as an honor student and earning a letter in lacrosse, he attended and graduated from Dixie State College in St. George, Utah. After earning a degree in engineering from Dixie State, Bob took a job with PG&E (Public Gas & Electric) and moved to Oakland, California. He read his company's diversity policy during his orientation and certainly understood that discrimination was wrong, but he had never been around so many openly gay people, and he felt uncomfortable. He didn't know what to say, so he often avoided working on team projects. Despite his discomfort, he was promoted to a managerial position within three years.

One day, Henry, one of his staff members, asked for a day off because his partner was sick. Bob said, "I never would've guessed you were gay! I mean, you can sleep with whoever you choose. Your sexual preference is your business, but I just didn't think that you were one of them." Bob was fired. He was shocked about being fired and thought that he was being kind and understanding during his conversation with Henry.

Bob's intention wasn't to offend Henry, but his lack of exposure to gay people and his monocultural vocabulary caused him to offend Henry and to lose his job. Even if Bob felt no ill feelings about homosexuality, he didn't have the skills to communicate effectively.

We've all been there. You may have wondered . . .

- My coworker is a Republican (or Democrat), and because she seems so smart, can I ask her how is that possible?
- Lots of Asians are good at math, so isn't that a compliment?
- Is it appropriate to use the term African American or black, Latino or Hispanic?
- My coworker just married his boyfriend. What do I call his new spouse?

You may not have negative feelings about a person's differences from you, but you may still not have the knowledge or language to act without causing them harm. Your life experiences have simply not taught you these communication skills.

AM I A BAD PERSON?

No.

We are uncomfortable—all of us—with difference. Being more comfortable with the familiar actually just means that we are human: we are biologically designed to have an unconscious preference for people similar to us.

Evolution made it so that we, as babies, would be wary of strangers. In other words, there is oftentimes an immediate physiological reaction to interacting with someone who is different from you.

The fear heightens because we oftentimes come into these situations with biases about those who are different from us. We fear our own biases: what they may make us say, feel, or do. We are scared of the "isms": racism, sexism, heterosexism, etc. We are terrified of being called an "ist": racist, sexist, or elitist. So we segregate and stay away from people who are different from us. We are uncomfortable with our discomfort. So like everything, the first step is to admit that sometimes you are uncomfortable around people who are different from you or those to whom you haven't been exposed. IT'S OKAY! WE ALL DO!

Look, I'm a diversity trainer, and I've made mistakes—tons of mistakes. I still make mistakes. I have been in situations where I didn't know the proper etiquette. I was eighteen years old before I knew that "gay" had a different meaning from "happy." I know that sounds unbelievable in today's world, but it's true. So when I started attending events of a dear friend (who happened to be gay), I didn't know how to refer to his significant other. Similarly, I am from a tiny town with a nonexistent Jewish population. When I started graduate school, I was completely inept at how to talk about holidays throughout the year. Do you wish someone a happy Yom Kippur, I wondered?

If we embrace the fact that we are ignorant in some areas, it opens us up to learning together. We are all in the same classroom. Most of us have the same objective: to get along with others. All we need is a little guidance.

So how do we learn?

Just like in any other classroom, we must ask questions and be open to learning. We are one another's teachers. I asked my gay friend how he wanted me to refer to his new husband. I asked my Jewish friends what was the proper greeting for Yom Kippur. I believe that people appreciate the willingness to learn.

I will never forget going to lunch eleven years ago with one of my good friends, Roya, who is white. I don't remember what we were talking about, but she said to me, "Is it black or African American? Which do you prefer because I'm confused about the whole thing, and I don't want to say the wrong thing." It was then I knew that we would be close friends. We were both comfortable learning and inquiring, so we avoided the "walking on eggshells" feeling that plagues some relationships or makes people avoid relationships with people who are different from them altogether.

Imagine you have a child who has been plagued with medical issues. On a respite from treatment, he gets invited to a birthday party. The hosting parent asks, "Are there any food or other sensitivities we should know about?" Would you be offended or flattered that she asked? Also, we feel more comfortable when we have a guidebook, a set of instructions. Right? Just like you learn more about another country before visiting it or about a new company before interviewing for a job there.

THIS GUIDEBOOK

It's also helpful in any classroom to have a guidebook: a reference to provide us with exactly how to engage with others. I had the opportunity to travel abroad as a teen. My travel guides always provided a tutorial of proper communication rules for that country. What has always struck me is how we do nothing to teach how to work together here in the United States, though we are a country of immigrants and diversity. This book is designed to serve as a comparable guidebook for navigating this unfamiliar territory and these uncomfortable issues. Its purpose is to assist us all in developing a culturally competent and compassionate communication style in an increasingly diverse world.

GUIDE? RULES? BUT CONVERSATION IS NATURAL. DO WE REALLY NEED RULES?

All of us already use rules in conversation. We have unconsciously been employing them almost from birth. (Pay attention to babies: they interact with other babies differently than they do with adults.) We talk differently to a person who is older than us than we do to a person younger than us; family members versus nonfamily members; strangers versus friends; a job interview versus a first date. Communication rules are both pervasive and useful.

WHO CAN REMEMBER ALL THESE RULES?

There isn't much to remember. You can say most things to most people. There are just some things that are almost guaranteed to offend. *Neversays* makes things simple because it provides you with a few things (when you consider the vastness of the English language) that you cannot say.

WHAT IS A NEVERSAY?

Neversays are things that you should not say under any circumstances.

SERIOUSLY? NEVER?

Yes, never.

WHY?

You have a higher than average chance of upsetting and/or offending the person you say the Neversay to. You also run the risk of getting reprimanded, expelled, or even fired.

Neversays are particularly important because these are phrases that people use frequently, and people are unaware that they are offensive. Many Neversays are said with the intention of making a connection with someone else but have the opposite effect. Neversays are phrases used by well-meaning people.

AREN'T YOU LETTING BIGOTS OFF THE HOOK?

Heck no. But the cause of most conflicts is that people just don't know another culture's vulnerabilities or codes of conduct, not that they are bigots.

I have a dear friend. Our kids play together all the time. Oftentimes my friend will call and say, "Where are your little monkeys (referring to my two boys)?" She is unaware that black people are sensitive about being called monkeys because of historical comparisons to them. She isn't racist, she is just ignorant about my sensitivity to that phrasing because of my race.

AREN'T WE ALREADY TOO PC?

Frankly, there is nothing political—or politically correct—about being respectful and kind toward others.

We don't hesitate to learn the rules of engagement when it's beneficial for us: we have applied for a job, so we learn the work culture's dress code, ensure we know how to give a proper handshake, and practice interview questions. When we have a crush on someone, we learn what their interests are, read their profiles online, and figure out how to best talk to them. And then if we get a date with our crush, when we meet their family, we speak more formally than we would normally because we want to make a good impression. But when learning communication skills that we don't view as directly benefiting us, suddenly, something feels too PC and requires too much effort. In fact, we unfairly put the responsibility of good interactions on other people: "they need to stop being so sensitive" or "they need to be able to take a joke."

AREN'T SOME PEOPLE JUST OVERLY SENSITIVE?

Yes, absolutely. That fact doesn't absolve us from being responsible for using offensive language. Additionally, who ultimately can judge? If someone is hurt or offended by something you say, the bottom line is they are hurt. Even if you are coldhearted and don't care about the other person's feelings, wouldn't it be nice to avoid the mess altogether by avoiding saying certain things?

I DON'T THINK ANYTHING IS WRONG WITH WHAT I AM SAYING

One time my uncle told me that childbirth wasn't that painful; women just needed to learn how to meditate and breathe. I won't repeat what I said back to him, but let's just say that I made it clear that no man, even if he were an obstetrician, could speak about the pain of childbirth. The same is true for groups trying to police their own conduct and measure the pain that they inflict on someone else. You must be willing to respect someone else's pain. Yes, it is convenient to police yourself, but it is ineffective—for you, for others, and for organizations.

Communication is ultimately about the receiver, not the speaker. What is the receiver's reaction to what you said?

WHY IS IT COOL FOR SOME GROUPS TO SAY THINGS AND NOT FOR OTHERS?

Put simply, membership has its privileges. Women can say things to other women that men can't, blacks to blacks, homosexuals to homosexuals, and so on. The only time that you can ever use "the group's language" is if you miraculously become a member of that group (note: just because you hang out with a group doesn't make you a member).

BUT IT'S COOL IF I'M IN MY OWN "GROUP" TO TALK ABOUT OTHERS—RIGHT?

Remember the "home rule." You do not know who someone has living at home with them. Their husband, wife, or child may be a member of the group that you are insulting.

NEVERSAYS PROMISE

———

In order to comfortably play any game, we must be aware of the rules. *Neversays* provides you with a quick list of phrases that many of us have been guilty of saying without realizing that others would find them offensive. Once you know these sensitivities, you can engage more comfortably.

Once we have a positive cross-cultural interaction, we will feel more comfortable interacting more and more and more (you get my drift). As the interactions increase, so will your relationships and productivity because you're now working in an inclusive environment, not just a diverse environment. You are now part of a true team—a true community.

What I hope happens is that as more people interact with people who are different from them, their biases are neutralized and their prejudices fade. People get to learn about individuals instead of myths about groups. If people use this book as a guide to communicate better and start working together more effectively, maybe real change will occur.

Let's get started . . .

NEVERSAYS

Neversays can typically be categorized into four types: Mr. Magoo Syndrome, Mayberrying, Assumption Dysfunction, and As(s)teism. The "Mr. Magoo Syndrome" is the suggestion that one cannot see, and is oblivious to, obvious differences in race, age, gender, ethnicity, and the like. The act of "Mayberrying" is believing that everything is perfect and that the experiences of all socioeconomic and cultural groups mirror yours. "Assumption Dysfunction" arises when a person assumes certain traits, actions, or beliefs based upon their preconceived notions of a group of people. And finally, As(s)teism is the dynamic of giving a backhanded compliment, essentially making a comment about a person or group that appears complimentary but actually insults the individual, their identity group, or both.

MR. MAGOO SYNDROME

Mr. Magoo Syndrome is when a person asserts that he doesn't see any differences in people or the way people are treated (e.g., "I don't see color" or "We all have some sort of disability"). On first examination, this approach to the world seems innocent, kind almost, as it implies the ideal that we are all the same. However, these assertions are unrealistic and disingenuous. We are not the same in the context of the realities of the world, so by denying the existence of any difference, Mr. Magoos actually highlight their discomfort with difference by saying that you don't see an obvious difference. One would never say that they don't notice a gender difference. A boy wouldn't say, "I didn't even notice that you were a girl." The gender difference may not affect your actions or decisions, but to suggest that you don't see gender at all is ridiculous and unbelievable. Mr. Magoo Syndrome provides a convenient, innocuous-sounding excuse for refusing to deal with something that makes all of us uncomfortable—dealing with someone who is different from us.

ASSUMPTION DYSFUNCTION (OR DISS-FUNCTION)

Assumption Dysfunction is when your statements are based on things that you have assumed about a particular group. Assumptions minimize your perceptions and worldview, blinding you to individuals and truths.

MAYBERRYING

Who remembers the idyllic town of Mayberry, USA, where all was good and pristine and Sheriff Andy, Aunt Bea, and Opie didn't have a care in the world? It was a place where everyone was kind and pleasant and every image and interaction was picture-perfect. "Mayberrying" is a term I came up with to describe people who desire to make everything perfect and to have all people conform to a narrow norm. These people gloss over anything inconsistent with their artificial utopian viewpoint. "Mayberrying" manifests in many ways, whether it's a refusal to recognize that bias and discrimination exist in society, refusal to acknowledge that they themselves have been insensitive, or the belief that the success of one member of a group can cure the injustices that impact the group as a whole.

AS(S)TEISM

As(s)teism arguably causes the majority of cross-group communication problems. What is "As(s)teism"? Asteism is when a comment is made that seemingly compliments an individual yet actually insults the individual or one of their identity groups. Many people are oblivious to this dynamic and only see the "positive" side of such comments.

Oftentimes with as(s)teism, there is no intention to harm anyone or to hurt feelings. This is why people who have made asteisic comments are left confused or even angry when they are confronted about their statements.

The two central roots of as(s)teism are ignorance and anxiety. Many people lack knowledge of the offensive nature of generalizations and their history of marginalizing minority groups. In addition, frequently, when people are uncomfortable or uneasy, they overcompensate by talking too much, saying too much and saying the wrong things.

THE NEVERSAYS

LAYOUT

For ease of understanding and use, this book approaches each Neversay in five ways:

1. We identify the Neversay and depict it in a cartoon designed to highlight the dynamic.
2. This is followed by a hypothetical real-world example of the Neversay in action.
3. We include the contrast between the words that are spoken and what is heard by the recipient.
4. We then seek to explore and explain the Neversay and the problems with the phrase.
5. And finally, in the "Flipside" section, we "flip" the Neversay and apply the Neversay in a different context or a different situation to help you make connection and be empathetic to a concept that may be unfamiliar to you.

No. 1

I Don't See Color

Wendolyn, 24 years old

In graduate school, I met a guy in in my biochemistry class. We started studying together at a coffee shop. Over time, we developed feelings for each other and talked about moving our relationship from friendship to dating. I asked him if the difference in our races caused him any concern (I am Latina; he is white). He said, "I don't see color." I was immediately turned off. Being Latina is so much of who I am. I wanted him to not only see a Latina woman, but also to appreciate a Latina woman.

What You Say	What People Hear
I don't see color.	I see color.
	I'm uncomfortable with your difference/race.
	It is easier for me not to acknowledge your difference.

Consider that according to a study, almost three-fourths of millennials believe that we should not see the color of someone's skin. Nearly 70 percent believe they have achieved this goal and are now actually color-blind, and (shockingly) the same percentage believes that we make society better by not seeing race or ethnicity.

Extra: Can you imagine what would happen to our court system if people really tried to say they couldn't see color? Ms. Smith, could you describe the assailant? Was he black, white, Latino? I don't know, I don't see color.

While the idea of being blind to one's characteristics is admirable, it's impossible and unrealistic. We see one another. We recognize if someone is male or female, black or white, tall or short. Study after study has proven that we actually see one another and form an opinion of a person within one tenth of a second—a blink of an eye. More specifically, according to a Harvard study, the first two things that humans notice about another human are race and gender.

What's even more interesting is that when humans are asked to only notice a person's gender and ignore their race, the part of the brain that recognizes race is still activated. So not only do we all see race, but we are also biologically programmed to see it.

Therefore, telling someone that you don't see color or that you are "color-blind" is disingenuous. Of course, you see color. Stevie Wonder sees color. When you say "I don't see color," what you are really saying is that "I won't acknowledge your race" or "It's easier for me not to deal with the difference," making it impossible to have an honest discussion or to form a trusting relationship with someone of another race.

FLIPSIDE

WHAT IF you had a large growth that covered the entire left side of your face. You tell your husband that you are seriously considering having the growth surgically removed. You have met with a highly reputable surgeon and were impressed with the results other patients had experienced in the pictures he showed you. When you asked your husband how he felt about it, he responded, "What growth? When I see you, all I see is perfection." While his response is sweet, would you also find it frustrating?

Quip Flipped

Neversay	Quip Flipped
I don't see color.	I don't judge you by the color of your skin or your race.
I'm color-blind.	I really try to see the whole person, not just a person's race.

No. 2

I Don't Care if She is Red,
Yellow, Purple, or Green

Stephanie, 44 years old

I was trying to talk to the principal of our school, who is also a close friend, about an African American colleague and friend who felt as if she had been passed over for the head of department position because she's black. Our school district is 98 percent white, and my black friend was one of just four minority teachers working in it. She had been working in the district longer than any other teacher in the English department. In response to my

---

concerns, my principal said, "I don't care if she is red, yellow, purple, blue, or green—I haven't made her the head because she isn't the right person for the job." I felt as if my principal were missing my point. I wanted him to deal with the facts: my friend was black, had seniority, was a highly rated teacher, and was hurt and angry. I knew that the school, or rather my principal, needed to deal with the situation so that my friend wouldn't quit, sue, or become ambivalent about her job; but I felt as if I couldn't even have a candid conversation with him because he wouldn't even deal forthrightly with my friend being black.

What You Say	What People Hear
I don't care if she is red, yellow, purple, or green.	I think race is just a matter of color.
	I don't want to acknowledge your race. It's easier for me not to.

The sentiment behind this statement is good. The speaker is attempting to get across that a person's race is inconsequential to their decision making. Unfortunately, while the sentiment is positive, the statement can generate negative feelings. Since there aren't red, yellow, purple, or green people, the statement belittles and distracts from the real issue, which is insulting when someone wants to be taken seriously.

This phrase also reduces race to something as simple as color when, for most people, especially minorities, race is much deeper than that. Reducing a social construct that has probably played a significant role in shaping a person's life's experiences into something as basic as color is insulting to them and signals that you are not prepared to absorb and deal with the issues being presented.

FLIPSIDE

WHAT IF you are a devout Christian and you are upset about your school's refusal to have the students recite "The Pledge of Allegiance" because it includes the term "God" in it, and some have argued that reciting it violates the First Amendment of the Constitution, calling for the separation of church and state. You attend a special school board meeting to address this issue because a large number of parents and teachers are upset. During the meeting, the PTA president says, "I don't care if you pray to God, Elmo, Santa Claus, or a Snickers Bar, prayer does not belong in schools." Can you see how this may offend the individual?

Quip Flipped

Neversay	Quip Flipped
I don't care if she is red, yellow, purple, or green.	I'm aware of the role race has historically played in the United States, but I have seriously considered this question, and my decision has nothing to do with race.
	I recognize that Janice is black and that there are cases where people do not receive jobs based on race, but that is not the case here.

No. 3

America is a Melting Pot

Frank, 38 years old

At every assembly, our school's principal talks about what a great melting pot our school is. I cringe every time she says it. We have students from over forty-seven different countries. I see all their differences. I love all their differences. I want to see them celebrated.

What You Say	What People Hear
America is a melting pot.	You must assimilate.
	You must lose your culture to mix in with the dominant culture.
	Your culture isn't valued or valuable.
	There is just one culture.

The melting pot is metaphorical for our society becoming homogeneous—a melting of cultures and nationalities together into a whole. The idea, at one time, was that immigrants would melt into one American culture. Unfortunately, when things are blended, the distinctiveness of each ingredient is lost. The term suggests that there is one culture that is superior to others and that immigrants and minorities should strive to assimilate to it.

Most will not embrace the idea of erasing one's culture. On the contrary, we all embrace family and cultural traditions. Think about what defines you, what makes you think of home. Most likely, it is your family's culture, traditions, celebrations that have been passed down from generations. No one wants to lose those distinctive characteristics by assimilating to one norm.

Nowadays, most people think of America being more of a salad, a tapestry or a mosaic of different cultures, where each culture is represented and respected.

FLIPSIDE

WHAT IF you started a job at a Fortune 50 firm, Delver Inc. The president of the company inherited the company from his father, and many of the company's executives are family members. The new president of the company, Mr. John T. Delver, makes an announcement that starting on Monday, each employee's last name will be Delver while at work to increase the idea of them all being one family and working toward one goal. How would you feel?

Neversay	Quip Flipped
America: The melting pot	America: The salad, kaleidoscope, stew, mosaic, tapestry, etc.

No. 4

There is Only One Race

– The Human Race

Rosa, El Salvadorian American, 22 years old

When I was attending Boston College, I roomed with five other girls. One time one of the girls brought in the mail and saw my magazine, *Latino Lives*. She handed me my mail and said, "First, I learn that you are a member of the Latino Student Union, and now *this*. I don't get why you have to subscribe to your *own* magazine. It's pretty racist, in my opinion, for you guys to separate so much. There is just only one race, the human race. We just need to all bond instead of separating."

What You Say	What People Hear
There is only one race, the human race.	I refuse to acknowledge your difference or that your difference has an impact on your life.
	We are all exactly equal, with equal opportunity, irrespective of our backgrounds.

"There is only one race, the human race" sounds like a beautiful slogan—a Hallmark card sentiment. When you consider that the two most unrelated humans on earth have a genetic similarity of about 99.68 percent in a lot of ways, saying that there is one race almost makes sense. Race, however, isn't a scientific attribute as much as it's a social construct, so the way a person experiences life is based on their visual, outward appearance. Making statements that ignore this dynamic doesn't erase someone's life's experiences; it only discounts them.

FLIPSIDE

WHAT IF after the primaries had ended in a highly contested presidential election cycle, the leading candidates of each party readied themselves for the debate. Each had unique platforms premised upon their party's core values. Jim Palmer of the Green Party was touting climate change, environmental regulation, and solar energy. Mabel Jennings of the Democratic Party shared remarks on universal health care, higher education subsidies, and tax increases on top wage earners. John Johnston of the Republican Party championed tax breaks and a stronger military and immigration reform. The fourth candidate, an independent named Charley Casserly, listened attentively. He then took the podium and said, "All these alleged differences in platforms and positions are nonsense! There is only one party, the United States Party!"

Quip Flipped

Neversay	Quip Flipped
There is only one race, the human race.	We are all in this together.
	We are one big mixed-up family.

No. 5

Don't Play the Race Card / Gender Card / Religious Card

Tina, 35 years old

I used to work for a small advertising firm. Oftentimes many of the best deals and contacts were made on the golf course. I was never invited to any of these outings, which I felt affected my sales. I went to the VP of sales to discuss this issue, and she said to me, "Listen, I'm a woman, and I made it. Don't try playing the woman card with me." To say that I was shocked is an understatement.

Extra

"What is more likely? That tomorrow will be called 'Thursday' or that Maxine Waters will play the race card in her ethics investigation?"
—Jonah Goldberg

Blacks essentially play the race card, when necessary as a counter to white privilege.

—Jonathan Coleman

What You Say	What People Hear
Don't play the race / gender / religion card.	I'm not listening to you.
	I don't believe anything you are saying is valid.
	I'm not considering your point.
	I think that you use your race / gender / religion opportunistically as an excuse.
	I don't see you as an individual, I only see your group.

When you say to a person that they are playing a card, you are implying that they are using their race, gender, or religious affiliation to take advantage of you or a situation or to gain sympathy or favor by conveniently pulling out a "card" whenever they choose. In other words, you are suggesting that whatever they say is invalid—merely a manipulative ploy. It is an attempt at dismissal of the person's feelings, claim, and integrity.

Do people make false accusations? Yes. However, it is often because they have been injured to the point that even the slightest misstep can be misunderstood. Instead of immediately shutting a person down, determine the issue and make an attempt to discuss it.

FLIPSIDE

WHAT IF your son goes to a prestigious private school where many of the parents don't work a standard nine-to-five schedule. In contrast, you work long hours and often don't get home until 8:00 p.m. You are constantly receiving emails to volunteer at your son's school and to drive to sporting events, etc. You have tried to explain to them that your schedule cannot accommodate doing things at the school. The teachers have been kind and moved parent/teacher meetings to later in the evenings. But every time you try to talk to the PTA president about moving some activities to accommodate you and several other parents, she always cuts you off by saying, "Listen, don't play that 'working-parent card' on me. We all have to do what we can to ensure we are there for our kids. Why should we give you special privileges?"

Quip Flipped

Neversay	Quip Flipped
Don't play the race / religious card.	Listen to the person's concerns.
	Ask why they think the treatment is attributable to race, gender, class, religion, etc.

No. 6

Who is the Husband, and Who is the Wife?

Gretchen, 44 years old

I was so happy when I finally was able to legally marry my partner of six years, Denise. I am a neonatal surgeon who works long hours. Over Thanksgiving, my mom asked Denise to help her in the kitchen. She said, "With all the hours that my daughter works, I'm assuming that you are the wife in the relationship."

What You Say	What People Hear
Who is the husband, and who is the wife?	One of you must inherently be "the woman," and one must inherently be "the man."
	I expect you to fit in with my marital standards.
	I'm not accepting your "concept" of marriage and expect you to fit into mine.

There is never an instance where it is appropriate to ask a same-sex couple who is the husband and who is the wife. Your question assumes that everyone lives the same and should fit into a set model of marriage. When two men have married, there are two husbands. For women, there are two wives. This is true regardless of who works outside the home, who earns more money, who is older, or who has primary responsibility for the kids.

Once legally wed, spouses—whether straight or gay—have earned the titles "husbands" and "wives." They may choose to call each other something else, but the right is theirs.

IN THE NEWS: The boyfriend of Michael Sam, the first openly gay football player to be drafted by an NFL team, was incorrectly called out by some as Sam's "wife" and "trophy wife" on social media, highlighting the traditional stereotypes of "husband/wife" roles.

FLIPSIDE

WHAT IF you are Jewish. You embrace your religion, and it is an important part of who you are. Your husband's family is Christian, and they celebrate Christmas. Every Christmas, your husband's family asks you what you want for your Christmas present. You are tired of the assumption that you should have the same beliefs and celebrate the holidays the same as them. It denies an important part of who you are.

Quip Flipped

Neversay	Quip Flipped
Who is the husband, and who is the wife?	To a gay man—husband.
	To a lesbian woman—wife.
	Ask "How would you like for me to refer to Mark?"

No. 7

Sexual Preference / When Did You Choose to be Gay?

WHEN DID YOU CHOOSE TO BE GAY?

Harrison, 29 years old

Monthly, the boss meets with us project managers to talk about new assignments and accounts. At our last meeting, my boss said, "Luke, we all are completely understanding of your sexual preference and that you have decided to live your life as a gay man, but I've decided not to put you on the Peterson's Worldwide account because they have a very conservative culture, which may cause some challenges to you." I knew that my boss was trying to be nice, but boy did he offend me.

What You Say	What People Hear
Sexual preference / When did you choose to be gay?	Sexuality is a choice.
	Homosexuality is not natural.

Choice is not a factor in sexual orientation. While scientists haven't come to a consensus as to all the factors that determine a person's sexual orientation, it is widely accepted that it is determined biologically. If there's anything that the science has taught us over the past few decades, it's that human beings have little—if any—conscious control over what arouses them.

When did you *choose* to be male or female, to be right- or left-handed, to be tall or short, to have a sensitivity to spicy foods? Exactly.

FLIPSIDE

WHAT IF you were born with Celiac's disease (an autoimmune disorder which causes the consumption of gluten, which is found in most common flours, to cause your small intestine to be severely damaged). When you attend company events or meetings, a special meal has to be prepared for you when they have sandwiches, pizza, pasta, etc. You always have to decline cake at office celebrations. During one of these parties, one of the secretaries (who knows about your condition and is oftentimes the one placing orders for food) comes up to you and inquires, "So when did you decide to become gluten-free? I mean you look great. It has clearly been great for your figure, but I don't know if I could do it."

Neversay	Quip Flipped
When did you decide to become gay?	It's a personal subject. Don't ask. If they want to share, listen. No one asks a heterosexual person, "So when did you know you liked the opposite sex?"

No. 8

Your Lifestyle is Your Business

Aaron, 41 years old

Our company started hosting a reception prior to the gay pride parade yearly. Although I am not gay, I attend the reception and parade in support of my friends. The day of the last reception and parade, I ran into one of my coworkers. I questioned, "Hey, are you headed to the boardroom for the reception?" He replied, "Naw, I don't understand all the hoopla.

I'm gluten-free, and I don't have to make a big deal out of it. Why do homosexuals have to? I don't announce who I'm sleeping with. Their lifestyle is their business."

What You Say	What People Hear
Your lifestyle is your business.	I don't want to talk about it or deal with it.
	I'm not comfortable with this subject.

It is difficult for most people to reveal that they are gay. According to a study by the Human Rights Campaign, a national gay rights group, 51 percent of gay, lesbian, transgender, and bisexual workers hide their sexual identity to most or all of their fellow employees.

Using the phrase "your lifestyle is your business" clearly indicates that you have no interest in discussing the issue any further and would prefer for the person to keep that information about their sexuality private. In other words, you are not comfortable and/or supportive of an aspect of this person's life. This statement automatically makes a person feel judged. Ask yourself if you would respond the same way if a person told you that they had decided to get married or to become vegetarian.

FLIPSIDE

WHAT IF you were a nursing mother. You didn't talk much about your kids at work because you just wanted to focus on getting the work done, and you largely kept your pumping needs at work to yourself. However, other employees have increasingly been using the lactation room as a break room to nap, eat their lunch, or to make a few calls. You stop by the office of Bob, one of the main offenders, to explain your schedule and need for the room. He responds simply that "Your lifestyle is your business" and returns to his work.

Quip Flipped

Neversay	Quip Flipped
Your lifestyle is your business	Say something such as "okay" to indicate that you have received the information (i.e., If someone tells you that they are a vegetarian, Muslim, or agnostic, you can simply respond "okay").
	Say exactly what you would say in response to whatever a heterosexual person stated about their relationship (i.e., "We are getting married." Your response: Congratulations).

No. 9

We All Have Some Sort of Disability

Erin, 62 years old

I have Asperger's syndrome. It makes participating in social situations difficult for me because I have trouble reading social cues. Hesitantly, I divulged my disability to my company shortly after I was hired. Consequently, they understand that I oftentimes will skip large meetings and after-work events. I was moved into an office instead of working in the cubicles like other staff on my level so that I could close my door and block out a lot of the noise and movement, which can be overwhelming to a person with Asperger's. A couple of my colleagues complained about me having an office when they were stuck in cubicles. Particularly because my disability is not something that you can see, they did not really believe or understand it. They would say things such as, "Well, heck, if Erin is disabled, then so am I. Where's my office?"

What You Say	What People Hear
We all have some sort of disability.	I am discounting your disability.
	I feel uncomfortable about your disability, so I'm going to act as if it's not a big deal.
	I am resentful of the accommodations you receive.

Many employers and colleagues do not understand how to best support a disabled person, which is problematic, considering that more than one in five adults in the United States is disabled. One in six people lose their job in the first year after acquiring an impairment; and less than half of workers with disabilities ask for adjustments to accommodate their disability as they did not want to draw attention to themselves. One third of those who revealed their disability said they received little or no help following their request.

In other words, being in the workforce with a disability is rare and difficult. When a person reveals that they have a disability, which many never do, they run the risk of being fired, ignored, or discriminated against, so you can presume that the majority of those who claim that they have a disability actually do. Their disability is not a choice or a characteristic they use to gain favor or special treatment that is unnecessary. You should respect the person, their disability, and the challenges they encounter and not discount their challenge by suggesting it is something we all face.

Quip Flipped

Neversay	Quip Flipped
Everybody has some sort of disability.	Let me know if and how I can best support you.

No. 10

I'm Not Racist, Sexist,

Homophobic, But . . .

When a sentence begins with "I'm not racist but . . ." or "I'm not sexist but . . .," there are very few positive statements that follow. Indeed, the speaker already knows this, consciously or unconsciously, which is why they lead the sentence with an apparent disclaimer. However, that disclaimer is meaningless when followed by a racist, homophobic, or sexist remark, which is almost always the case. For example: "I am not sexist, but I just don't think female firefighters have the strength to do the job." It is akin to "No offense but . . ." statements, which almost universally offend.

What You Say	What People Hear
I'm not racist, sexist, homophobic, but . . .	I'm racist.
	I'm sexist.
	I'm homophobic.

EXTRA – If one of your colleagues begins a sentence with "I'm not . . . but . . .," tell them not to say anymore. It is okay to cut someone off and voice that you would prefer not to participate in gossip or bad talk in the workplace.

FLIPSIDE

WHAT IF you grew up in Long Beach, California, and now work and live in Santa Monica. Since you can remember, you've enjoyed everything that your state had to offer—from long summer days at the beach to LA Lakers games, to skiing in Tahoe, and to enjoying San Francisco food crawls. Your friends and family largely all live in California, many having returned after brief stints elsewhere. You are sitting at an airport bar in O'Hare, awaiting a return flight to LAX, when the traveler on the stool next to you turns to you and says, "I don't necessarily hate Californians, but . . ." How would you feel?

Neversay	Quip Flipped
I'm not racist, sexist, homophobic, but . . .	There is no replacement. Do not open a statement this way. Pause and rethink the substance and delivery of the sentiment you intended to express.

No. 11

I Don't Think of You as (a Person With Disability, an Asian, Gay, Etc.)

Morgan, 43 years old

As the VP of HR, I was in charge of managing a sexual harassment complaint filed by one of the company's employees. I had to meet with the president of the company to bring him up to speed on what was happening with the case. So he says to me, "What do you think about this suit? I don't really even pay attention to a person's characteristics so much. Like you, Harriet, I don't even think of you as a woman. As far as I am concerned, you are one of the boys."

The phrase "I don't think of you as" immediately demonstrates discomfort on the part of the speaker with whatever group is being addressed (LGBT, Asians, blacks, Jewish, females) and further serves to denigrate that group by asserting that the recipient is somehow better than or "above" that group. It inherently suggests that all people with disabilities, members of a racial minority, gay people, etc. share identical behaviors and traits and are part of a monolithic whole. It also expresses that the speaker is more comfortable with the recipient's traits than those of the group. While often spoken with good intentions, this opening is a red flag for discomfort with a given race, gender, or sexual orientation.

What You Say	What People Hear
I don't even think of you as . . .	I'm refusing to see the difference.
	I am uncomfortable with the difference.

FLIPSIDE

WHAT IF you were promoted at work. You are now the boss of people who had been your colleagues and close friends for twenty years. After your promotion, your friends treat you the same and completely ignore your assignments and emails. One of them says to you, "We don't even think of you as the boss. You are still just one of us in our eyes."

Quip Flipped

Neversay	Quip Flipped
I don't even think of you as	I am so comfortable with you . . .
	I oftentimes forget . . .
	Your———is just one more characteristic that I like about you.

No. 12

You are Too Sensitive /
Can't You Take a Joke?

What You Say	What People Hear
You are too sensitive. / You can't take a joke.	You are weak.
	I don't respect your feelings.
	Your hurt feelings are invalid.
	You aren't the victim. *Since* you are accusing me, I am actually the victim.

"You are too sensitive" is a classic "It's you, not me" response to someone who has voiced hurt over something you have said. By saying it, you are rejecting any possible responsibility for hurting or offending someone. You are minimizing (and actually attempting to erase) the emotional damage you have done to someone else. It unfairly places all the blame for a situation squarely on someone else's shoulders.

Tip: If someone makes you the butt of their joke—respond with, "That's not a joke, and it's not funny to anyone, except to someone who is insensitive to others."

A joke is something that is funny to both the speaker and the recipient. If it is only funny to the speaker at the recipient's expense, it's not a joke—it's bullying. Actually, when you say that another person is too sensitive, it means that you are actually insensitive because you are placing your feelings and enjoyment above someone else's. You are establishing yourself as the final arbiter of humor. You are saying that as long as you are receiving joy, it doesn't matter how anyone else feels.

FLIPSIDE

WHAT IF you went to a restaurant for a special occasion. You weren't seated until thirty minutes after your reservation. The waitress was rude to you and your guest. You asked for your steak to be cooked medium rare, but it was almost burned. Your guest's food didn't come out until fifteen minutes after yours. After an hour, the hostess came to your table and told you that the next reservation was waiting so you would need to vacate the table soon. Frustrated, you go to the manager to complain. You list all the atrocities you have had to endure that evening. The manager says to you, "Your expectations are simply unreasonable. Look around, everyone else seems happy."

Neversay	Quip Flipped
You are too sensitive. / You can't take a joke.	I'm sorry.

No. 13

Where are You Really From?

Jake, 39 years old

My dad is Jamaican and Irish, and my mother is Japanese. I swear there is not a day that goes by that I don't get asked where I am from. I always answer "Boston" because that is where I was born and raised. I still live there today. I have a thick Bostonian accent. At least 80 percent of the time, people respond with "No, where are you really from?" It's as if they feel that Americans can't look like I do.

What You Say	What People Hear
Where are you from for real?	You don't look American.
	You don't fit in into my ideal of America or of what an American is.

Immigrants account for 13 percent of the 316 million total US residents. Adding the US-born children (of all ages) of immigrants means that approximately 80 million people (or one quarter of the overall US population) are first- or second-generation Americans. These statistics demonstrate our diversity and why Americans look different from one another. There is no "American-looking" person. There is no typical "girl-next-door" look. Don't assume that someone wasn't born in America because they look different from you or from your ideal of how Americans look.

We are curious beings by nature. It's understandable that you would be curious to know the heritage of someone who looks very different from you. But consider the diversity of the United States and ask yourself, would you ask a blond-haired, blue-eyed person the same question about their background? If not, why? Only 2 percent of the world's population is blond, and only one in six Americans have blue eyes.

Another reason people find these kinds of questions awkward is they don't consider their origin "small talk" (although often people who barely know you will ask the question). Some ask, "What is the motivation behind the question? Why do people want to know where I was born within five to fifteen minutes of meeting me? Why do you feel the need to dig deeper into my ancestry/ethnicity? What does that information provide for them—a compass of how they should treat me—if I belong or not?"

FLIPSIDE

WHAT IF you spent the past ten years going to college, medical school, and completing your residency. You are a highly credentialed surgeon at one of the most prestigious medical centers in the country. En route to a medical conference, you wear casual traveling clothes of jeans and a hooded sweatshirt. Your seat companion starts up a conversation with you and soon asks what you do for a living. You respond that you are a thoracic surgeon at Alta Linda Medical Center in Palo Alto. Your seatmate responds with a look of disbelief, stating, "No, no, really . . . I'm serious . . . what do you do for real?"

Neversay	Quip Flipped
Where are you *really* from?	What's your heritage?
	What's your background?
	Just don't ask.

No. 14

I Never Would've Guessed

that You are Gay, Black, Etc.

What You Say	What People Hear
I never would have guessed that you are—	I have a stereotype for your identity group of people and their behaviors.
	I don't see you as an individual. I see your group.

When you say to a person that you never would've guessed they were gay, black, Republican, etc., you are saying that you have assigned certain characteristics to that group and expect everyone in that group to ascribe to the same look or behaviors. Using phrases like "I never would have guessed that you are" dehumanizes a person in that you are applying the same method you would to describe an animal, e.g., an elephant has long trunk, is gray and large; a Chinese person is quiet, smart, and short.

It is difficult to form even a working relationship with someone whom you feel has prejudged and classified you. Underlying assumptions kill the possibility of two people getting to know each other.

FLIPSIDE

WHAT IF you are a female and a senior in high school. During the last month of school, the honor society hosts an award banquet. You win the science scholar of the year award. One of your male friends comes up to you and says, "I never would've thought that you were so good in science. I thought girls were more into English since you like to read all those novels, poetry, and everything."

Quip Flipped

Neversay	Quip Flipped
I never would have guessed that you are . . .	There is no flip. Steer clear of this phrase and sentiment.

No. 15

Your People are So . . .

Tom, 22 years old

I was a celebrated track star in high school and college. My senior year at Notre Dame, after a year of dating my girlfriend, I went to visit her parents for Christmas. Lillian was bragging about my accomplishments, including that I was captain of the debate team and was about to graduate Summa Cum Laude, when her father commented, "Your people are such great athletes."

What You Say	What People Hear
Your people are so . . .	When I see you, I only see your one identity group.
	I don't see you as an individual.
	Your accomplishment came easy because it's a natural gift.

Once you use the phrase "your people," you have informed the person you are talking to that you are not seeing them as an individual but as a group. You also have indicated that you have tagged this group with certain characteristics.

The problem with such statements is that, irrespective of what follows, your introductory phrase has applied a generalization to a racial, gender, ethnic, or other identity group. Even though in the abstract being told that one is athletic, intellectual, sensitive, flamboyant or hard working may be viewed as a genuine compliment, these generalizations minimize the individual's identity and ascribe homogenous traits to a group that may or may not fit. They also assign traits to a person that they don't personally value or identify with (i.e., the female vice president in corporate America may not want to be viewed as "nurturing").

A final problem presented by "your people" statements is that they immediately create a division between the speaker and listener. By implicitly drawing the distinction between "your people" and "my people," the statement creates a gulf along lines of race, ethnicity, gender, or sexual orientation.

FLIPSIDE

WHAT IF you worked hard all through high school to get straight As, to get involved in extracurricular sports and activities, and to do community service. You were determined to get into Harvard, and you did. *That* was the easy part. You then busted your tail while at Harvard, including too many all-nighter study sessions, to graduate at the top of your class. You land a plum job at Goldman Sachs upon graduation. On the first day of new analyst orientation, one of your colleagues whispers, "You know the chairman is from Harvard—you Harvard alums have it made. Just show up and you'll be successful." You were offended as his comment denigrated all your hard work.

Quip Flipped

Neversay	Quip Flipped
Your people . . .	You are . . .

No. 16

You Aren't Really / You are Different

Lisa, 37 years old

Most of my life I have been the only minority in a group of white females. Many times they've said to me, "You are not really black," or "I know you are black, but you are 'different.'"

These statements have left me wanting to scream, "'Them' is me! I am black! If that is how you feel, what do you think about black people generally?"

What You Say	What People Hear
You are not like them. / You are different. / You aren't really . . .	I don't accept your group.
	I think your group is inferior.
	I would prefer to think of you not belonging to that group.
	I ascribe certain characteristics to your group.

Telling someone—even in the form of a compliment—that they are different from their identity group is an insult to the person and to their identity group. First, the statement indicates that you have stereotyped and assigned a specific group of characteristics to a person's identity group. Second, the statement implies that you have made a negative judgment about that group. Last, you are now saying that the person with whom you are speaking to is superior because they don't subscribe to the typical characteristics of that group. Without question, it's insulting.

FLIPSIDE

WHAT IF you are a computer programmer. You love your field of work and your colleagues. One day the HR department asks you to participate in a subcommittee that is organizing a team-building event. The HR director says to you, "We thought that you would be perfect for this committee because you aren't like the rest of the IT department. You actually have a personality."

Neversay	Quip Flipped
You are not like them. / You aren't really . . . / But you are different.	You don't need to address difference at all. Simply tell the person what you like about them.

No. 17

You are a Credit to Your Race, People, Profession, Kind

Jeff, 42 years old

I had to travel a lot as a consultant, which required me to use the corporate card and report my expenses. When I would buy a drink with dinner or purchase a movie, I would ensure that I reimbursed the company for those expenses. We all turned in our expense reports weekly to our CFO. One day, in the elevator, I ran into our CFO. He said, "Jeff? You are the most ethical, responsible, honest person in this company, or actually in any company I have ever worked with. You complete your expense reports perfectly. You are a credit to your people." At first, it felt good to be complimented by one of the executives, but as the day progressed, I started to feel as if the CFO felt that being ethical was an anomaly for a Jewish person.

What You Say	What People Hear
You are a credit to your race, kind, profession, family.	I don't think highly of your race, kind, profession, family.
	I have low expectations of your kind.

Ask yourself this question: Would you ever say to a white person "You are a credit to your race"? Similarly, why is it acceptable to say to a lawyer "You are a credit to your profession" and not to a doctor? Aren't there bad and good ones in both professions? It's simple: If what you are saying degrades another group, then it is not a good thing to say. There are no exceptions.

Saying that someone is a credit to something also suggests that there is a master scorecard tracking all groups.

FLIPSIDE

WHAT IF you lived in a thirty-floor condominium complex with over a dozen units on each floor. Hal, the doorman, has worked there for several years and greets each tenant by name with a smile each morning and night. When you come down to the lobby one morning, the elevator doors open, and you see a candy wrapper on the floor from the Halloween festivities the prior night. You pick it up and deposit it in the trash on the way to the door. Hal opens the door for you, gives you a quick wink, and says, "Mr. Hoxall, you are a credit to the seventeenth floor!"

No. 18

Wow, Your English is So Good /
You Have No Accent

Dan, 57 years old

My family immigrated from Vietnam when I was two. My dad started a
sausage business in 1970 which has grown to employ around one hundred
people in our small town. We made the decision recently to contract out
the delivery arm of our business to deliver our sausages to the markets and
restaurants in the state. When we met with one of the potential contractors,
the president of the company said to me, "You speak English so well, and
you don't even have an accent. Where did you learn it?"

"Home," I replied. "Just as I suspect you did."

We decided not to do business with that company. We don't need to work with small-minded people.

What You Say	What People Hear
Wow, your English is so good. / You have no accent.	I only expect white people to speak well.

When you are shocked that someone doesn't have an accent, it means that you believe Americans look one way. This statement suggests that you think that anyone who is brown is an immigrant or visitor to the United States.

FLIPSIDE

Imagine you are the Chief Medical Officer of a large hospital system. You attained this position through years of Ivy League studies and over twenty years of exemplary performance as a surgeon. Just before checking in to a medical conference in New York you run into a couple of women from your undergraduate pre-med club in the lobby. You greet them casually with a "what's up" and quickly reminisce about the old days of tailgating, frat parties and drinking too much. As you proceed to the counter and give her your last name, she casually says: "Welcome MRS. Johnson, we are looking forward to hosting you and Dr. Johnson." You quickly correct her that it is YOU who is the Doctor. She apologizes profusely, stating: "I am so sorry, you just didn't SOUND like a doctor!"

No. 19

You are So Articulate

Erik, 24 years old

More than twenty times over the course of my time at Princeton, I was told by surprised people how articulate I was. I never heard my white friends saying this to one another, only to me, as if they assumed I would speak using Ebonics since I was African American and that it was a forgone conclusion that a white person would speak proper English. I was tempted to remind them that I was attending Princeton—an Ivy League—just as they were.

EXTRA

"I mean, you got the first mainstream African American who is articulate and bright and clean and a nice-looking guy. I mean, that's a storybook, man."

—Joe Biden, describing fellow candidate Barack Obama. The remark was made the same day Biden filed the official paperwork to launch his presidential campaign. Biden later apologized and said the remark was taken out of context.

Saying that someone is articulate, a rather odd compliment, is rooted in the assumption that the person wouldn't be articulate. You must question why you wouldn't expect a person to speak well. Is it because of her race, socioeconomic level, level of education, geographic location? Many times people will be shocked that a person from the South doesn't "speak country" or a person from an urban area doesn't use slang. Their surprise is insulting because it illustrates that they have stereotyped the other person.

FLIPSIDE

WHAT IF you were interviewing at a large trading company in Manhattan. You hand the interviewer your impressive resume. After the interviewer reviews it, he says, "You are a woman, *and* you can code? You shouldn't have any problems getting a job here."

No. 20

One of My Best Friends Is . . .

Sandra, 21 years old

I was hanging with my friends Marie and Amy after work. We had known one another for years and enjoyed our Thursday night drinks tradition. Before too long, Marie noticed another group of friends that she knew and invited them over to join the table. As we made introductions, one of the new people, Mark, said, "It's great to meet you, Sandra. One of my best friends is Latina." It made me uncomfortable as Mark had not addressed anyone else's race. It also gave me pause about how "comfortable" Mark was with minorities if he had to make the point of addressing it. It made me feel compartmentalized as simply "the Latina," as if Mark saw nothing more. It turned me off immediately, and I quickly said goodbye to Marie and Amy and headed home.

What You Say	What People Hear
One of my best friends is . . . / I once dated a . . .	I am uncomfortable with our difference.
	That one characteristic is all I see when I see you.
	I desperately need you to know that I'm cool with the difference in us.

The "one of my best friends is (e.g., gay, Asian, black, Latino)" statement is a way of legitimizing the authenticity of one's attitude on diversity. Some individuals feel compelled to align themselves with acquaintances or "friends" of another group as a way of giving themselves more cultural capital. Unfortunately, the "one of my best friends is" statement, although intended to convey the speaker's comfort with diversity, only makes their true discomfort more obvious.

FLIPSIDE

WHAT IF you are white. You meet a new colleague who tells you within the first thirty minutes of meeting her "My doctor is white. We have a great working relationship."

Quip Flipped

NEVERSAY	QUIP FLIPPED
One of my best friends is . . .	Don't say anything. No one wants your social resume.
I once dated a . . .	

No. 21

When are You Going to Have

Kids? / But You Have Kids

Alice, 44 years old

Alice had been working at Amalgamated Steel since graduating with her business degree twenty-two years ago. She had steadily worked her way up from her entry accounting position. She loved her job and loved the "game" of climbing the corporate ladder. She had excelled in every role and was the youngest person in company history to be named vice president and senior vice president respectively. While happily married, her husband was equally career-focused. While they had discussed having children on a number of occasions, neither was particularly interested, and they had decided to remain childless. At work, one of the two executive vice presidents had announced his retirement. Alice was on the short list for the promotion. When the chairman called Alice to his office, she was confident it was about the new role. However, he asked her to sit down and said pointedly, "Alice, when do you plan to have kids? You've got to be at least forty, and time may be running out for you." Alice was incredulous. She knew he would not ask any male counterpart the same question and felt diminished and marginalized. She also wondered if concerns about a maternity leave and parental responsibilities were factoring into the chairman's decision.

What You Say	What People Hear
When are you going to have kids?	You are a woman. You are expected to have kids.
But you have kids?	Your commitment isn't really to this company.
	You will only be here a short time before you leave for maternity leave or motherhood.

It is wrong to assume that all women want to or will have children. It is also a personal decision and topic that shouldn't be asked in the workplace. The question suggests that the expectation is that a person's career or job is either not important to them and is quite possibly temporary.

FLIPSIDE

WHAT IF you are turning sixty in a few weeks. You come to work one day to have the HR manager introduce you to a thirty-year-old man. The HR manager says that she would like for you to train the new employee in the next few weeks to do your job. You later ask the HR manager if the company is expanding or if you hadn't been doing your job well because you are wondering why there needs to be two of you doing the same thing.

She responds, "Oh, we just figured that you would be retiring soon. You turn sixty in three weeks."

Neversay	Quip Flipped
When are you going to have kids?	There is no replacement. Asking someone about their personal life and family plans is inappropriate.
But you have kids?	

No. 22

You Must Be PMS-ing / It Must Be that Time of the Month / Menopause

Catherine, 33 years old

The early 2000s were tough on our company. We went through a series of layoffs, which made everyone on edge. No one felt as if their job was safe. Looking back, I must admit that I too was tense. I pushed the people I managed even harder because I wanted our department to look good so I could retain all my staff. I wrote a rather terse memo to our group, reprimanding them for sloppy work on a project. Shortly after seeing my memo, one of my direct reports came into my office and said, "Whoa, are you PMS-ing or something? That note was over-the-top. You are so irrational sometimes."

What You Say	What People Hear
You must be PMS-ing.	You are a woman. Thus, your performance and behavior isn't reliable or consistent.
It must be that time of the month.	You are acting this way only because of a physical problem. It isn't because of anything I did wrong or a conscious decision.
Are you going through menopause?	You are not in control of your emotions.
Your hormones …	You are incapable of handling stress.

When you reduce a woman's behavior, decision making, and leadership to changes in her physical state, you are questioning her ability to be a stable, consistent, and competent employee, colleague, or boss. You are also implying that men are better performers because they don't have the same hormonal makeup.

FLIPSIDE

WHAT IF you are working in a fast-moving Fortune 200 tech company. Things are usually fairly stressful because the market is extremely competitive. You are running a meeting when you discover that some of your staff failed to complete a critical task. Admittedly, you raised your voice and reprimanded all the staff rather harshly. After the meeting, one of the other managers comes up and says to you, "Boy, you really let them have it. I guess you haven't had sex in a while. You seem super tense."

Neversay	Quip Flipped
You must be PMS-ing.	You seem stressed. Let me know if I can help or support you in any way.
It must be that time of the month.	
Are you going through menopause?	
Your hormones . . .	

No. 23

Do You Know How to Use Technology, Email, Twitter?

Carl, 62 years old

I have worked with the same catalogue company for forty years. I used to be in the mail room but have slowly worked my way up. For the last ten years, I have worked in the marketing department. We are trying to reach a younger audience so have started placing ads on Facebook and

Instagram and Tweeting about our promotions and products. I wondered why I was being left off some project teams, so I asked the manager if she hadn't been pleased with my work or something. She said to me, "Honestly, Carl, we are now really trying to use technology to penetrate the twenty- to thirty-five-year-old market. I assumed that you would be uncomfortable working on developing marketing strategies that used technology as a medium."

What You Say	What People Hear
Do you know how to use Twitter, email, etc.?	I don't think that you are qualified for your job.
	Old people are not capable of performing in today's work world.
	Young people are more capable than the old people.

It is wrong to make assumptions about someone's skill set based solely on their age. Additionally, it's oftentimes inaccurate. Today 35 percent of adults sixty-five and older use social media.

FLIPSIDE

WHAT IF the company where you worked started an intramural basketball league as another way of team building. You didn't even know about it until you read the company newsletter encouraging employees to come and support the team, as they were in the adult league championships. You asked your cubicle mate about the league and why they hadn't asked you to participate. He says that he figured since you were only five feet eight inches that you didn't know how to play basketball.

What You Say	Quip Flipped
Do you know how to use Twitter, email, etc.?	Tell me your skill set, strengths, and weaknesses
	In what areas are you interested in working/focusing?
	Let me know if you have any questions.

No. 24

When are You Retiring?

Jack, 59 years old

My wife died six months after I retired as an accountant in the post office and from the army. At that point, I thought it would be a good idea for me to start working again. I was so bored and lonely just sitting around the house all day. Because of my military and government background, I was hired by a fairly small company that created a software for deployed military to track packages that were mailed to them overseas. Every now and then, during my first three years at the company, someone would ask me when I planned on retiring. I didn't know if my job performance was bad or if they were just trying to get rid of me. I loved my new job and felt as if I was just getting started there.

What You Say	What People Hear
When are your retiring?	You don't belong here.
	You are old.
	I don't see your value.

Some find discussions about age or related to age inappropriate in personal relationships; so of course, these types of conversations and questions are completely inappropriate in business relationships.

FLIPSIDE

WHAT IF you were working as an English teacher. You adored working with the kids, seeing them connect with the literature, and watching their writing skills improve. Every now and then, your mother-in-law would ask when you were going back to school to get your administration degree so that you could become a principal. You do not want to, nor have ever stated that you wanted to get into administration. Every time she asks you this question, it makes you wonder if she doesn't think that you are a good teacher, teaching doesn't pay well enough to support your household, or isn't a respectable enough job.

Quip Flipped

What You Say	Quip Flipped
When are you retiring?	None. Don't say it.

No. 25

Man Up / Grow Some Balls

Pete, 30 years old

My coworker Jerry is such a pushover. Every Friday, our boss Frank comes to his cube around 4:45 p.m. with an "emergency" project. Each time Jerry works all weekend only to find out on Monday that he had been given a false deadline—there was no emergency. I knew this upcoming weekend was Jerry's daughter's graduation. Once again, Frank stopped by at 4:30 p.m. and asked him to work over the weekend. He mumbled a bit but reluctantly agreed before coming over to my office to complain. I told him he needed to grow some balls and tell Frank to find someone else.

What You Say	What People Hear
Man up. / Grow some balls.	Masculine traits are more effective than feminine traits.
	You are weak.
	Women are weak.

The phrases "man up" and "grow some balls" suggest that women are the weaker gender. It is often used to shame men into doing a task that requires strength or courage. These terms dismiss whatever the person is saying and tells them they need to get over it.

FLIPSIDE

WHAT IF you are a man who manages fifty employees. A lot of your time is spent managing the personal conflicts between your staff and ensuring that they work well as a team. During one of the mediations you are conducting between two employees, one of them says, "You can't really empathize with the dynamics in this office because you don't have a soft, nurturing side. Part of the problem we have is that you are incapable of seeing the human side of things because you are a man."

What You Say	Quip Flipped
Man up. / Grow some balls.	Get it together.
	Let's talk about why you are finding this situation challenging.

EPILOGUE

When I moved from Northern Virginia to San Francisco, California, my husband and I went to several "welcome" dinners. I quickly noticed that it seemed everyone in San Francisco ate masterfully with chopsticks. Few ate with chopsticks back in Northern Virginia, whereas here, it is so assumed that you are proficient with chopsticks that many restaurants don't even bring you flatware (and there is something shameful when you ask). So I would sit at many meals attempting to eat with these foreign objects. I'd stab my food, reconfigure the chopsticks multiple times, accidently drop them, and drop tons of food on myself and on the table. While I am sure I looked foolish, no one—not my hosts, not the restaurant staff—took offense at my blunders. They may have been laughing inside, but they didn't see my fumbling as an insult to Asians. Why?

People knew that my chopstick challenges weren't because of a lack of respect for other cultures but to a lack of exposure. I was incompetent but not insincere in my efforts. They trusted my intent. I was a good woman who was bad with chopsticks. I assert that trust is what is lacking in most of our cross-cultural relationships. Without trust, you cannot have a positive interaction. I have to be trusting that the restaurant I enter will welcome me, that the server will treat me fairly, and that my colleagues will not ridicule me for my lack of chopstick skills. The restaurant must trust that I will pay my bill and act appropriately when I'm in the restaurant; the waiter must trust that I will tip him aptly for good service; and my colleagues must trust that my incompetence with the chopsticks does not speak to my appreciation of the culture. We act differently when we don't trust someone, a group, or a situation. We also can sense when someone doesn't trust us, and we react accordingly. Think about the issues between residents in urban areas and the police. If the residents don't trust the police, and the police don't trust the residents, you have the perfect makings for disaster: two armed groups acting defensively.

What you must understand is that fear has a boomerang effect and knocks everyone down on its way out and back. You act poorly because you are fearful; people fear you because you are acting poorly. Humans sense fear just as dogs do. When a dog senses fear, only then will he attack. The same can be said for humans.

Though we display our fear differently, it is all still fear. Categorizing people the way one does music makes us feel in control of a varied, chaotic world filled with a plethora of personalities, tastes, styles, races, cultures, religions, sexual orientations, gender affiliations, etc. Wouldn't it be calming if all the bad people looked one way and all the good people looked another—just like in the movies? But life and people aren't that simple. Similarly, wearing rose-colored glasses and acting as if there were no differences, conflicts, or "isms" in this world is also counterproductive. If ignorance is truly bliss, it is so only temporarily. You will bump against the truth, hurting yourself and others.

It's exhausting and incredibly limiting being angry, scared, or defensive all the time, isn't it? It's exhausting and incredibly limiting to pretend that the world and people are mono-lithic. Both approaches are clearly ineffective and typically destructive. Look at us. Look at our world.

What if you decided to trust? What if you made the decision that for the time you have in this world, you are going to live it with your arms opened instead of crossed, your eyes opened instead of closed? You will trust that most of the people in this world are good. I'm not asking you to be naïve. There are some real jerks out there—some are evil and dangerous. But most people are well-meaning, well-intentioned, and yes, oftentimes in many ways very different from you.

So the majority of the world, regardless of race, gender, sexual identity, size, disability, income level, political affiliation, etc., is filled with people who have two important things in common: we are decent; and we are flawed.

If someone says something to offend you, assume that the person is ignorant, not evil. What if you took the opportunity to go from hurt to healed, from being a reactor to an educator. What if we took instances where people say the wrong thing to move from hurt to healing?

I am suggesting that we enter into all relationships, from the one-hour relationship you have with your server at the restaurant to the eight-year relationship you have had with your boss, the same way you do any friendship or romantic relationship with the knowledge that this person will make mistakes and may say things that may injure you. You can use those times to move on from hurt to healed by being a teaching moment as opposed to a fractious one.

We are on this planet together. We are working together, shopping together, and going to school together. That is not going to change. There are no outs. You cannot vote out, move out, stomp out, out-earn, out-strategize, or outrun diversity. So I suggest that we all actively figure out how to best get along with your neighbors, classmates, and colleagues. Just like with any relationship, we need to trust, communicate, and learn the things that promote unity and the things that we should simply *never say*.

Printed in the United States
By Bookmasters